3800 13 0028844 0

HI

D0237983

# Think of a
# BEAVER

HIGHLAND
LIBRARIES

WITHDRAWN

For Willie Llewellyn
K.W.

For Lotte Manning
M.M.

First published 1993 by Walker Books Ltd
87 Vauxhall Walk, London SE11 5HJ

This edition published 2010

2 4 6 8 10 9 7 5 3 1

Text © 1993 Karen Wallace
Illustrations © 1993 Mick Manning

The moral rights of the author and illustrator
have been asserted

This book has been typeset in Bembo Educational

Printed in China

All rights reserved. No part of this book may be reproduced,
transmitted or stored in an information retrieval system in any form
or by any means, graphic, electronic or mechanical, including
photocopying, taping and recording, without prior
written permission from the publisher.

British Library Cataloguing in Publication Data:
a catalogue record for this book is available from the British Library

ISBN 978-1-4063-1860-9

www.walker.co.uk

# Think of a
# BEAVER

## Karen Wallace

### illustrated by Mick Manning

WALKER BOOKS
AND SUBSIDIARIES
LONDON · BOSTON · SYDNEY · AUCKLAND

HIGHLAND
LIBRARIES
380013002884h0
WITHDRAWN
£4.99

Think of a beaver.

Bright-eyed beaver, brown and bushy,
hurries to the stony lake shore.

Beaver breath is hot and woody –
he's grunting, puffing, dragging branches.

Beaver teeth are sharp as chisels,
orange like an autumn pumpkin.

Beaver teeth can cut through trees, and
grow again when beaver breaks them.

Beaver hands are monkey clever.
He builds a lodge

from mud and branches,
tunnels in from under water.

Beaver feet are webbed like ducks' feet,
push like paddles through the water,
past the slowly swimming salmon,

down to where the tangled roots
lie buried in the reedy lake bed.

Beaver tail is flat and scaly,
like a rudder under water,

like a trowel for mud and branches,
carefully curled and carried safely.

Beaver
tail
sounds
danger
warning.

He whacks it
SLAP!
upon the water.

Other beavers
hear the message...

Quickly dive!
Protect the
young ones!
Find the tunnel
under water!

Beaver kits are born in May-time,

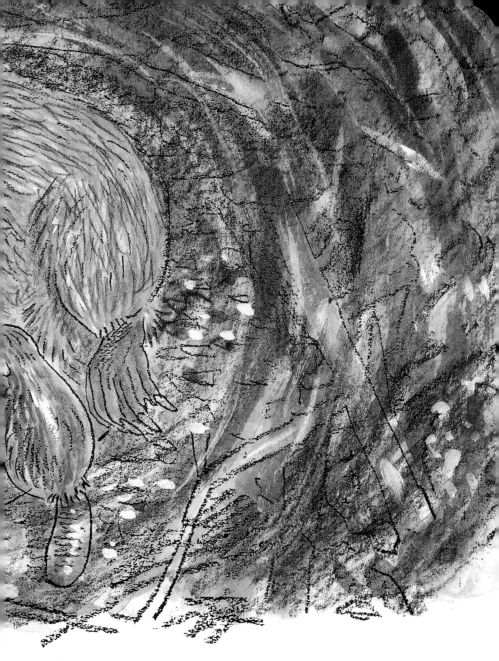

dry and warm on wood-chip bedding.

They cry like children
when they're hungry.

They learn to swim
along the tunnel,
through the water
to the lodge roof.

They play
like children
in the sunshine.

Brainy beaver, engineer now,
cuts canals through boggy meadows.

He chooses trees beyond the shore,
chops them down and floats them home.

When the days are growing colder,
leaves are falling, red and yellow,
busy beaver's work is hardest.
He gathers wood for winter eating,

for when the ice is hard as iron.
He plasters mud and sticks together,
mends his dam, protects his shelter
against the cold and snowy weather.

Bushy beaver's warm in winter.
He doesn't mind the icy water.
He grows two coats

to keep the cold out –
thick and silky on the skin side,
rough and rainproof on the outside.

All winter long, while snow is falling,
when birds have flown and bears are
sleeping, beaver lives inside his lodge room,
warm and dry on wood-chip bedding.

He nibbles at his sunken branches,
combs his fur and waits for spring.

Think of a beaver.

# More about beavers

Beavers eat lily roots. They also eat bark and young wood from aspen and birch trees.

On land beavers are quite clumsy, but in water they are swift and streamlined. A see-through membrane protects their eyes while they're swimming, so they can see under water. A beaver can swim for a quarter of a mile without coming up for air.

Beavers dam streams with sticks, stones, roots and mud to make a pond.

Beavers usually build their lodge in the middle of the pond. They leave spaces in the roof to let in air. Most beaver lodges have at least two tunnels.

Beaver feet are useful for grooming.

Beavers greet each other by chattering ...

and nibbling each other's cheeks.

Beavers live in families. Couples mate for life and work together. Baby beavers are called kits. A mother beaver usually has two to four kits at a time.

The beavers in this book live in North America, but there are beavers in Europe and Asia as well.

# Index

## About the Author

Karen Wallace was raised in a log cabin in the woods of Quebec, Canada. She says, "When I was a child, I sometimes saw beavers building their lodges on flooded land. Their bright eyes and busy ways were quite wonderful and will stay with me forever."

## About the Illustrator

Mick Manning has written and illustrated numerous books for children, often working with his wife, Brita Granström. His book *A Ruined House* was chosen by the Children's Laureate, Quentin Blake, as one of his fifty favourite books. Mick and his family live by the sea in Northumberland.

There are 10 titles in the
**READ AND DISCOVER** series.
Which ones have you read?

 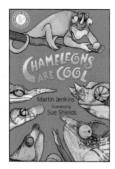  

 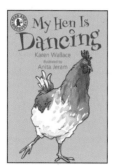  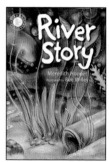

Available from all good booksellers

www.walker.co.uk

FOR THE BEST CHILDREN'S BOOKS, LOOK FOR THE BEAR.